Steiner   3738
* Jack Is Glad, Jack Is Sad

DATE DUE			
Feb 1, Sally		room 17	
DEC 15 1965 2-16		2-16	
DEC 22 1965 2-16		2-16	
FEB 19 74	K3	2-14	
2-17	MAY 1 '76		

BY THE SAME AUTHOR-ARTIST

These are all Borzoi Books for Young People
published by Alfred A. Knopf

JACK IS GLAD JACK IS SAD

JACK IS GLAD

JACK IS SAD

WRITTEN AND ILLUSTRATED BY
CHARLOTTE STEINER

ALFRED A. KNOPF NEW YORK

3/38

L. C. Catalog card number: 62-14765

THIS IS A BORZOI BOOK,
PUBLISHED BY ALFRED A. KNOPF, INC.

Copyright © 1962 by Charlotte Steiner

The sun is shining,
It's no longer dark,
When Jack's new puppy
Wakes him up with a bark.
Jack is <u>glad.</u>

But when his puppy runs away,
One morning on a rainy day,
Jack calls and whistles and looks all
    around;
But the puppy has gone and cannot be found.
    Jack is <u>sad</u>.

When neighbor Freddy
Comes skating by,
And Jack tries to trip him
To make him cry—
Jack is <u>bad.</u>

Jack and Freddy start to fight,
And Jack goes home a dreadful
 sight.
His mother says, "Son, no
 circus for you!"
And Jack well knows she
 means it, too.
 Jack is <u>sorry</u>.

The circus parade has come to town,
With elephants, horses, and a funny clown.
Jacks runs with the others down the street,
But "No circus," says Mother when they meet.
Jack was <u>hopeful</u>.

Jack helps with the dishes,
Obeys his mother's wishes;
Goes to bed at eight
And tries not to be late.
Jack is <u>good</u>.

So Jack goes to the circus, and sees Maybelle,
The pretty girl who rides so well.
He likes the clowns and the dancing bear,
But he can't keep his eyes from Maybelle's
golden hair.
Jack is <u>charmed</u>.

When Jack wakes in the night
And can't see a light
But hears from the ground
A mysterious sound —
Jack is <u>frightened</u>.

Jack runs to the window,
Leans out and shouts "Hey!
Who's making that noise?"—
Sees the cat slink away.
Jack was <u>brave</u>.

Jack and Anne dance together
And to their surprise,
At the fair in the park
They win the grand prize.
They are <u>proud</u>.

Jack visits Granny and eats too much cake;
Awakes the next morning with a big tummyache.
He scolds little Bee, his puppy he chases,
And at his good mother he makes naughty faces.
Jack is <u>grouchy</u>.

When Jack plays tag with sister Bee,
And Bee falls down and hurts her knee,
Jack dries her tears. "It was just a fall.
Come, take my hankie—please don't bawl."
Jack is <u>gentle</u>.

Jack takes peanuts to the zoo;
The elephant likes peanuts too.
Jack shows him one, then pulls it away,
And the elephant covers him with spray.
Jack was <u>mean</u>.

When Jack's friend Anne whispers
In Eleanor's ear,
And Jack listens hard
But must not hear—
   Jack is <u>jealous</u>.

One day from a rowboat
Jack lands his first fish!
He'll have it for supper,
Baked in a fine dish.
Jack is <u>happy</u>.

The runaway puppy now finds its way back,
Tired and hungry, its white coat turned black.
Jack feeds and bathes it, makes it look snappy;
His pet has returned and now Jack is . . . _____

When their little kitten climbs way up high,
Bee and Anne are ready to cry.
Jack brings it back to a cheering crowd.
Mission accomplished—Jack is . . . ——

Jack didn't listen when teacher read,
But giggled and pulled Peggy's hair instead.
"Jack, stay after school," says stern Miss Lorry.
It's easy to guess that Jack was . . . _____

For Anne's birthday Jack's gift has a bright
    pink bow—
Anne opens it up and screams, "Oh, <u>oh</u>!"
A white mouse jumps out—what a terrible scene!
All the girls think that Jack is . . . _____

The new boy next door comes out one day.
Jack offers his truck: "Do you want to play?"
"Come ride my pony," says the friendly lad.
Sharing is fun—both boys are . . . ———

Text set in Bodoni Regular. Composed at Lettick Incorporated, Bridgeport, Conn. Printed by Philip Klein, New York. Bound by H. Wolff Book Mfg. Co., New York. Paper manufactured by S. D. Warren Co.